US ARMED FORCES

UNITED STATES ARMY

KENNY ABDO

abdobooks.com

Published by Abdo Zoom, a division of ABDO, P.O. Box 398166, Minneapolis, Minnesota 55439. Copyright © 2019 by Abdo Consulting Group, Inc. International copyrights reserved in all countries. No part of this book may be reproduced in any form without written permission from the publisher. Fly!™ is a trademark and logo of Abdo Zoom.

Printed in the United States of America, North Mankato, Minnesota.
092018
012019

THIS BOOK CONTAINS RECYCLED MATERIALS

Photo Credits: Alamy, AP Images, Everett Collection, iStock, ©Keith McIntyre p23/ Shutterstock.com, ©US Army p6,14/CC BY 2.0, ©US National Guard p12,16/CC BY 2.0
Production Contributors: Kenny Abdo, Jennie Forsberg, Grace Hansen
Design Contributors: Dorothy Toth, Neil Klinepier

Library of Congress Control Number: 2018946302

Publisher's Cataloging-in-Publication Data

Names: Abdo, Kenny, author.
Title: United States Army / by Kenny Abdo.
Description: Minneapolis, Minnesota : Abdo Zoom, 2019 | Series: US Armed Forces | Includes online resources and index.
Identifiers: ISBN 9781532125515 (lib. bdg.) | ISBN 9781641856966 (pbk) | ISBN 9781532126536 (ebook) | ISBN 9781532127045 (Read-to-me ebook)
Subjects: LCSH: United States. Army--History--Juvenile literature. | Armies--Juvenile literature. | Military departments and divisions--United States--Juvenile literature.
Classification: DDC 355.00973--dc23

TABLE OF CONTENTS

United States Army 4

Intel 8

In Action...................... 16

Glossary 22

Online Resources 23

Index 24

UNITED STATES ARMY

With boots on the ground around the world, the United States Army has fought for more than 240 years with bravery, sacrifice, and **determination**.

The US Army's **mission** is to protect the United States of America from any outside threat through strategy and specialized training.

INTEL

The US Army is older than the United States of America. The Continental Army was formed in 1775. After defeating the British during the **Revolutionary War**, the United States of America was formed on July 4, 1776.

The Corps of Discovery was a unit of the United States Army. They were lead by Captain Lewis and Second Lieutenant Clark. They mapped out the **Louisiana Purchase**.

The US Army has three parts. They are **Active Duty**, Army National Guard, and United States Army Reserves.

The **active duty** soldiers work full-time, 12 months of the year. Reserve soldiers have a military role with a civilian career. They fight whenever they are needed, but are not full-time.

IN ACTION

There are half a million active soldiers in the Army today. They are **deployed** around the world.

Many US Presidents have served in the Army. Dwight D. Eisenhower was a General. He was on **active duty** between 1915 and 1969, except for his two terms in office.

There are more than 3,000 Military Working Dogs (MWDs) in the field today. Among their many duties, they help find hidden explosives before they can be detonated. MWDs have saved many soldier's lives.

GLOSSARY

active duty – full-time service in the armed forces.

deploy – the act of moving soldiers into a position of action.

determination – the method of establishing something precisely.

Louisiana Purchase – land the United States purchased from France in 1803.

mission – an important job carried out by the armed forces.

Revolutionary War – a war fought between England and the North American colonies from 1775 to 1783.

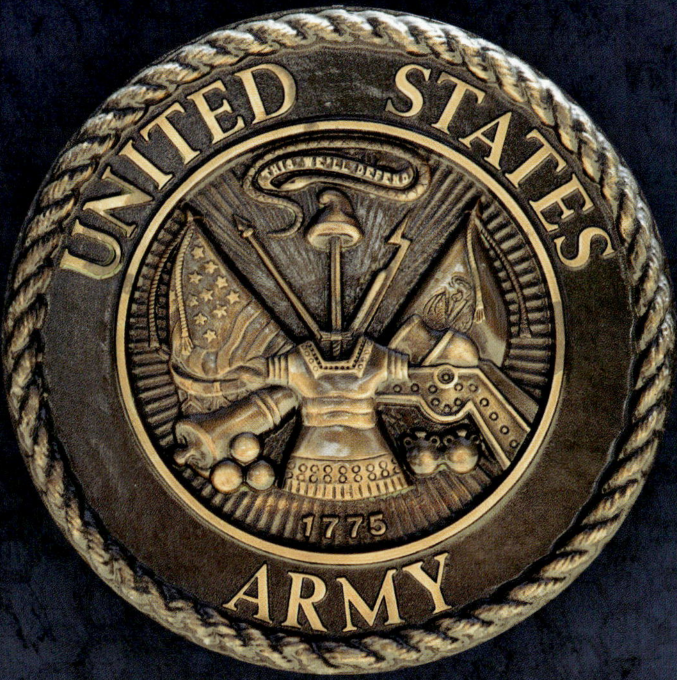

ONLINE RESOURCES

To learn more about the Army, please visit **abdobooklinks.com**. These links are routinely monitored and updated to provide the most current information available.

INDEX

active duty 12, 15, 16, 19

Clark, William 10

Continental Army 9

Eisenhower, Dwight D. 19

formation 9

Lewis, Meriwether 10

Louisiana Purchase 10

Military Working Dogs 21

mission 7

National Guard 12

Revolutionary War 9

training 7